The Puddle

DAVID McPHAIL

 HOUGHTON MIFFLIN   BOSTON • MORRIS PLAINS, NJ

California   •   Colorado   •   Georgia   •   Illinois   •   New Jersey   •   Texas

For my little brother and his ducks

Houghton Mifflin Edition, 2005

Printed in China

ISBN-13: 978-0-618-06195-2
ISBN-10: 0-618-06195-9

16 17 18 19 20-SDP-09 08 07

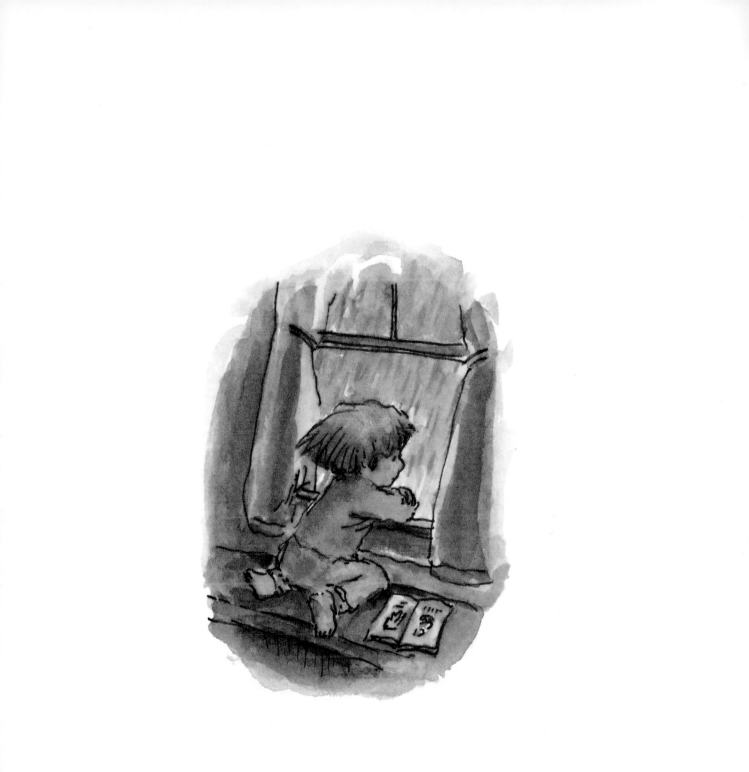

It was a rainy day.

I asked my mom if I could go out and
sail my boat in the puddles.
She said, "Okay, but *you* stay out of the puddles."

I got dressed in my rain boots and coat,

and went to sail my boat

in the largest puddle I could find.

A frog came along and sat down beside me.

"Nice boat," he said.

Then he jumped onto my boat and

sailed away. "Come back!" I called, but he wouldn't listen.

A turtle floated by.
"Teatime," said the turtle. "Care to join me?"

"I can't," I said. "I need to get my boat back. Besides,
I'm not allowed to go in puddles."

But the frog steered my boat right into the turtle. CRASH!
The frog laughed. He thought it was funny.

The turtle didn't think it was funny at all. She was angry.

Then an alligator offered to help.
"Want me to get your boat back for you?" he asked.

"Really? That would be *great*!" I said.

So the alligator swam out

to take my boat away from the frog.

He did.

But the boat looked different than it did before.

"Sorry," he said.

"Don't worry about it," I told him.

Next, a pig wanted to swim in the puddle.

He took a running start,

jumped in, and

splashed me.

"My mom's not gonna like this!" I yelled to the pig.

Before long, a thirsty elephant showed up.

She drank . . .

. . . and drank . . .

. . . until the puddle was nearly gone.

The other animals were upset with the elephant.
"Put back the water!" they shouted.

So she did.

She left, and

when the sun started to come out, the other animals left, too.

Then the sun dried up the rest of the puddle.

I took my boat home.

When I got there, my mom had a hot bath waiting for me.

"Can I bring my boat?" I asked her.
"Of course," she said.

And I did.